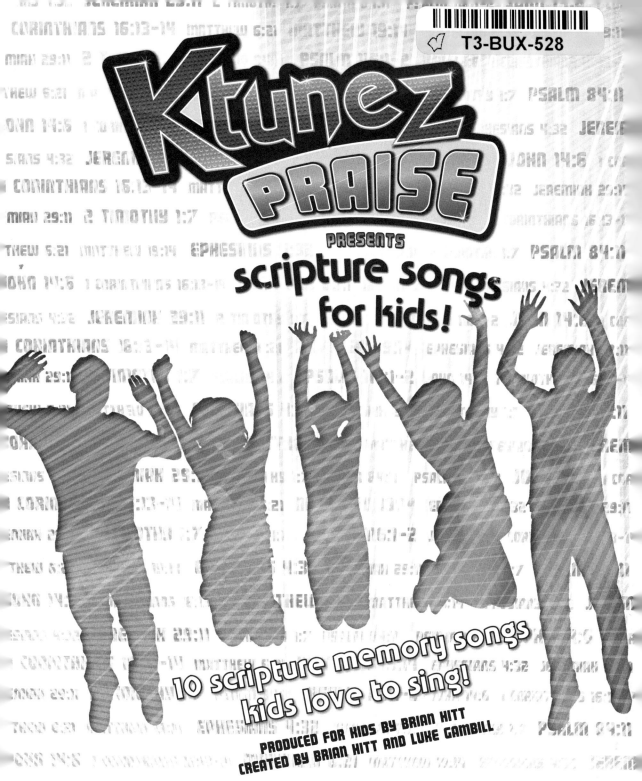

Ktunez PRAISE

PRESENTS

scripture songs for kids!

10 scripture memory songs kids love to sing!

PRODUCED FOR KIDS BY BRIAN HITT
CREATED BY BRIAN HITT AND LUKE GAMBILL

AVAILABLE PRODUCTS:

www.brentwoodbenson.com

 a division of  BRENTWOOD-BENSON
music publications

CONTENTS

NOTE: Quoted Scripture in the lyrics of the songs is in a ***Bold Italic*** font.

Ephesians 4:32

(ESV)

Words and Music by
BRIAN HITT, MICHAEL FORDINAL
and APRIL GEESBREGHT
Arranged by Brian Hitt

Driving rock (♩=91)

N.C.

Eb5   Bb5

Ab5   Bb5   Eb5   Bb5

CHOIR

What a

When some-one makes you sad, feel bad, it's a drag.

Ab5   Bb5   Eb5   Bb5

drag.

When you trip and fall, and you hear them laugh, you

Ab5   Bb5

4

10

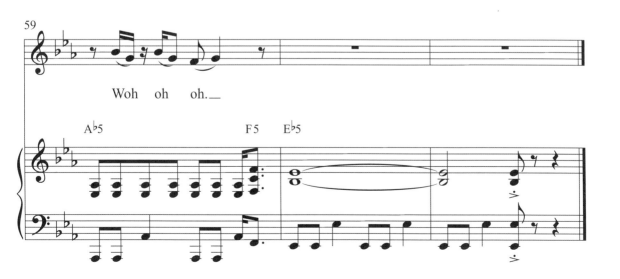

Jeremiah 29:11

(Jeremiah 29:11-13 NIV)

Words and Music by
BRIAN HITT, MICHAEL FORDINAL
and JAMES TEALY
Arranged by Brian Hitt

14

know the plans I have for _____ you," de - clares the _____

LORD, de - clares the LORD. "For I

know the plans I have for _____ you," de - clares the _____

LORD, de - clares the LORD. "Plans to

LORD.

2. When I ___ de - clares the

LORD.   "Then

you will call on Me and come and

18

Keep Alert
(1 Corinthians 16:13-14 NAS)

Words and Music by
BRIAN HITT, JAMES TEALY
and STEPHEN DUNCAN
Arranged by Brian Hitt

24

30

No Fear Anthem

(2 Timothy 1:7 ESV)

Words and Music by
BRIAN HITT, TYRUS MORGAN
and JAY SPEIGHT

Arranged by Brian Hitt

36

shamed. God's a - live and strong.

We're not a -

fraid, we're not a - shamed.

God's a - live and strong.___

Sun and Shield
(Psalm 84:11 NASB)

Words and Music by
BRIAN HITT, MICHAEL FORDINAL
and SUE C. SMITH
Arranged by Brian Hitt

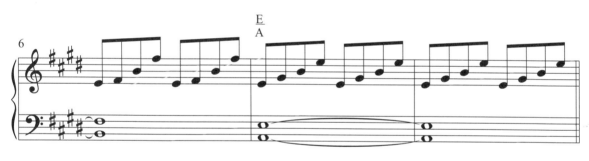

You're the sun that shines___ in the dark - ness,

45

46

52

As Long as I Have Breath

(Based on Psalm 116:1-2 NLT)

Words and Music by
BRIAN HITT and JAMES TEALY
Arranged by Brian Hitt

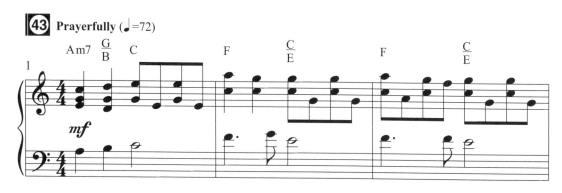

I love the LORD 'cause He hears my voice

and my prayer for mer - cy. I love the LORD 'cause He

Woh,_____ woh,____ woh._____

'Cause He bends down to lis-ten, I will pray as

long as I have breath!

The Way
(John 14:6 NIV)

Words and Music by
BRIAN HITT, TYRUS MORGAN
and JAY SPEIGHT
Arranged by Brian Hitt

Lyrics:
Don't let your hearts be, don't let your hearts be trou-bled, trou-bled. You be-lieve in God,

60

62

I'm_____ gon - na save_____ you a place,

Je - sus said:___

mel. **I am the Way, and the Truth, and the Life. No one**

___ comes to the Fa - ther, ex - cept through Me.

66

Come to Me
(Matthew 19:14 NIV)

Words and Music by
BRIAN HITT and JAMES TEALY
Arranged by Brian Hitt

Treasure
(Luke 12:34 NIV)

Words and Music by
BRIAN HITT, MICHAEL FORDINAL
and APRIL GEESBREGHT
Arranged by BRIAN HITT

CHOIR

You could put your trea-sure in a car or

send it in a rock-et up to Mars.

78

oh. — Don't you know? Don't you know?

Don't you know? There your heart___ will be al - so.

___ will be al - so. Woo!

The Books

Words and Music by
BRIAN HITT, MICHAEL FORDINAL
and APRIL GEESBREGHT

Arranged by Brian Hitt

Gen-e-sis, Ex-o-dus, Le-vit-i-cus, Num-bers, Deu-ter-on-o-my,

Josh-u-a, Judg-es, Ruth. I'll learn them all; it's so eas-y.

84

Es - ther, Job, Psalms and Prov - erbs, Ec - cle - si - as - tes

Cm

Song of Songs, I - sa - iah, Jer - e - mi - ah's proph - e - cy.

Cm
Eb

Lam - en - ta - tions, E - zek - i - el, Dan - iel, and Ho - se - a,

F7

Joel and A - mos, O - ba - di - ah; Jo - nah in the whale, and then it's

Cm

25 Mi-cah._____ Oh yeah, it's Mi-cah._____

Cm

28 — Na - hum, Ha - bak - kuk, Zeph-a - ni - ah,

B♭   Cm

31 Hag - gai, Zech-a - ri - ah, Mal-a - chi — i - i - i - i. From the

B♭   F(no3)   f

34 Old   to the New it's not   fic - tion, it's a   fact. It's the

A♭   E♭   B♭

f

88

My First PIANO BOOK
worship songs & Hymns

Only $14.99 each

Beginner Piano Arrangements by David Thibodeaux

* **Volume 1 - Worship Songs**

* **Volume 2 - Worship Songs**

* **Volume 3 - Worship Songs**

* **Volume 1 - Hymns**

* **Volume 2 - Hymns**

DISCOVER MORE GREAT KIDS MUSICALS

FROM THE BRENTWOOD KIDS MUSIC CLUB!

Down by the Creek Bank

Can you believe it? Down By the Creek Bank is 25 years old this year! It's a timeless Classic for kids of all ages! Introduce a new generation to Down By the Creek Bank and watch your kids have even more fun than you did 25 years ago! So, grab a fishin' pole and a friend and join us for the most fun 35 minutes anyone can have "by the old, holler log!"

The Tale of Three Trees

The Tale of Three Trees brings to life this children's Classic - a story of some trees with a dream, and a God with a plan. Through the hopes and dreams of three trees, we are reminded that even when we can't see the forest for the trees, there is no prayer too big or too small for God!

We Are United

Unify your children's choir as they "survive" the challenges of Henotes Island in We Are United, a musical island adventure featuring fun original songs your kids will love performing. Based on the 1 Corinthians 12:12-27 theme "one body, many parts," six castaways compete on the island to win the "grand prize," only to discover that the real way to win is to work together as one in Christ.

JOIN

THE BRENTWOOD KIDS MUSIC CLUB

AND RECEIVE OUR NEW MUSIC RELEASES FOR AN ENTIRE YEAR FROM TOP ARRANGERS: DENNIS & NAN ALLEN, JEFF SANDSTROM, RHONDA FRAZIER, ED KEE, ANNETTE ODEN, JOHNATHAN CRUMPTON, LUKE GAMBILL, PAM ANDREWS AND MANY MORE!

As an exclusive member of this amazing Kids Music Resource, you will receive:

• A wide variety of new, energetic and exciting Kids music delivered straight to your door 4-5 times each year. This includes seasonal and non-seasonal musicals, collections and great DVD resources for Kids Choir, VBS, Summer Camp or Sunday School. **(That's over $150.00 in music!)**

• Complete songbooks, audio recordings and DVD samplers – no excerpts!

• 15% discount on all choral books, listening CD's and CD/DVD accompaniment tracks.

• Share the Music magazine containing new release information, informative articles, activities and games for your kids, teaching tips and special offers for Brentwood Kids Music Club members only!

• Choral Music Specialists available to assist you with product information.

• 24 hour on-line ordering with special offers exclusively for club members.

• A FREE music voucher for purchase of music product!

CALL 1-800-846-7664 TODAY
AND LET US DO ALL THE WORK FOR YOU.
WE WILL ONLY SEND YOU OUR VERY BEST!

BOBKCCTEN